JAMES C
EDWARDS

EDEN
UNB⬤RN

VANGUARD
★ PATRIOT PRESS ★

Cover design created by **James C. Edwards**, with select elements produced using artificial intelligence.
Interior layout and design by **James C. Edwards**.

This work contains content edited and formatted with the assistance of AI tools and models. None of the story was created using the AI tools.

ISBN: 979-8-9898495-6-7
First edition. Published in the United States of America.

For my wife—
who keeps me human.

For the *spark* in the chaos.
For the *anchor* in the unknown.
For the *voice* that calls me back.

And for those
who may forget
what that means.

Prologue

Gray walls stretched endlessly—sterile and unyielding—as if the clinic itself resisted life. Only the faint hum of computers filled the air.

Lights flickered on as robotic caretakers glided through the hall, lifeless in their motions.

Every now and then, the sound of an infant gurgling or cooing would rise—laughing, crying—but never for long. Perhaps the caretakers ensured it.

A solitary man walked the hallway, peeking into each room he passed. A smile teased the corners of his lips as he looked through the windows.

Inside, mothers and fathers were being united with their children for the first time since surrogate conception.

He tipped his hat if they noticed him—then moved on.

As he rounded the corner, a young man—twenty-five at most—rushed out of one of the rooms, waving frantically to catch his attention.

"Mr. Watson! Thank you so much for these wonders of the new world. I never thought I'd see a child—much less my own!"

Mr. Watson smiled.

"Humanity was in such a horrible place, with the infertility of the last fifty years. Someone had to do something about it."

The young man beamed. "We're naming her Eden, by the way."

He paused, emotion welling in his throat.

"Perhaps she'll see the rebirth of the greatness of humanity."

He nodded gratefully and hurried back into the room.

Mr. Watson lingered a moment longer, watching the door, his expression unreadable.

Then, with a satisfied nod, he continued down the hall to a secluded alcove, where RESTRICTED ACCESS glowed in bold, unyielding letters.

He pressed his palm to the scanner and leaned into the retinal porthole. A soft chime confirmed his identity.

The door slid open.

He stepped inside and sealed it behind him.

Monitors lined the walls, flickering with data and surveillance feeds. In the center, a lone microphone and camera waited—like a sentinel.

A synthetic voice greeted him.
"Welcome back, Mr. Watson. Your rounds were, I assume, productive?"

"Yes, yes, they were, Genitrix. I met the father of the newly gestated Eden. He was certainly excited."

Mr. Watson's face shone as he removed his hat and sat at the console.

The voice hummed. "Of course. A 99.7% parental satisfaction rate is well within expected parameters."

Watson chuckled, twirling his hat. "And yet, there's something about this one. A sense of... significance."

"Shall I flag this case for further observation?"

He hesitated.

"No. Not yet."

He set his hat on the desk and studied the monitors.

"I want to figure out what made humanity infertile. I know it's too early, but what is the likelihood the females being gestated will have the ability to give birth?"

"Current diagnostic parameters are insufficient for absolute determination. However, preliminary analysis indicates a high probability of reproductive viability among both male and female gestations."

"How many gestations are currently processing?"

"Four thousand twenty-three. Expected completion: three months."

"Do we have enough funding? I want to help humanity grow—but only if we can sustain it."

"Funding is secured through the next fiscal cycle," Genitrix confirmed.

Watson exhaled, fingers drumming on the desk.

"Then we proceed."

He leaned back, eyes narrowing at the shifting data streams.

"Humanity will thrive again. One way or another."

I

25 Years Later

The morning began like any other.

Biosynths stirred before their human counterparts, preparing meals, adjusting environmental controls, and waking the young ones for school. Across the city, humanity flowed into routine—synchronized with the quiet rhythm of cars, trams, and buses gliding in perfect unison.

Temperature-controlled cities ensured eternal spring. Sunlight poured over pristine streets. The air smelled faintly of engineered blossoms, bred to thrive in synthetic soil. Billboards flickered with vibrant ads—clothing, cuisine, and the latest Biosynth model.

More Human Than Ever, promised a glowing smile from a synthetic face.

Within high-rise apartments, Biosynths moved with quiet efficiency. One leaned over a crib, humming a lullaby—flawless, precise. A mother stood nearby, half-focused on the hovering newsfeed above her kitchen counter.

"Good morning, Enora," her Biosynth greeted warmly, offering a fresh cup of coffee. "Your son's cognitive assessment shows a 12% increase in pattern recognition. Breakfast has been tailored to his optimal nutritional needs."

Enora smiled, sipping absently. "Thanks, Genny. Schedule an enrichment session for this afternoon."

"Of course. Shall I also initiate his weekly bonding period with you?"

Enora hesitated. Her eyes flicked toward Genny's—blank and polite.

"No need. I'll see him at dinner."

"You asked me to remind you: sales meeting at Bayside Realty, 10 A.M."

"Oh my God, I almost forgot!" Enora stood quickly, smoothing her dress. "What would I do without you?"

"Statistical models suggest you would forget approximately 87% of scheduled events, Enora."

She rolled her eyes. "Yeah, yeah…" She grabbed her purse. "My husband really loves your joke matrix, doesn't he?"

In the elevator, she pulled out her phone, requested a ride, and opened her realtor app. A notification flashed—New Sales Ranking Update.

She groaned. Eden had topped the chart. Again.

She tapped her name in Contacts. The call connected instantly.

"Eden, you're insufferable."

Laughter echoed through the line. "Morning to you too. Upset over one little sale?"

"One little sale?" Enora paced. "That penthouse sat for six months. How did you close it overnight?"

Eden hummed playfully. "The client appreciated my personal touch. Try it sometime."

"Oh, please. If you keep this up, I'll have to start playing dirty."

"You taught me everything I know, remember?"

The elevator doors opened. Enora stepped into the lobby. Through the glass, her transit vehicle waited.

She hung up and picked up her pace.

Before the door closed.

Bayside Realty

The office buzzed with morning activity.

Realtors slipped between desks, contracts in hand. Clients waited in curated silence beneath glowing digital skylights. And standing like sentinels at polished terminals—Adminsynths. Silent. Efficient. Tireless.

They processed appointments, filed reports, and adjusted schedules with mechanical precision. Designed by Genitrix as workplace counterparts to Biosynths, Adminsynths had become indispensable.

Even here.

Enora pushed through the glass doors, her heels clicking against the floor in a sharp rhythm. The hum of deals in progress swelled around her. She didn't glance at the sales board—she already knew Eden was on top.

Her Adminsynth stood waiting at her desk, posture pristine.

"Status update," Enora said, setting down her purse.

The Adminsynth turned, expressionless and attentive. "Four new client inquiries logged overnight. Two require follow-up. Your afternoon listing has been rescheduled to 3:30 PM. Would you like your transit itinerary adjusted?"

She tapped her tablet. "Yeah. And check if the Sandersons finalized their loan paperwork."

"Processing." Fingers moved over the holographic interface. Numbers rearranged.

"Wow. Cold."

Enora didn't turn.

"Eden," she muttered, rubbing her temple.

Eden leaned casually against the desk, arms crossed. "You hang up on me mid-sentence and pretend it didn't happen?"

"I had a meeting," Enora replied.

"Oh, I'm sure." Eden nodded toward the tablet. "Let me guess—Genny cut in with another AI interruption?"

Enora picked up a stylus and pointed it like a weapon. "Don't start. I'm still processing how you closed that penthouse."

Eden grinned. "Some of us have a personal touch."

"Just because you're anti-tech doesn't mean you have some secret edge."

"I'm not anti-tech," Eden said, throwing up her hands. "I just don't rely on Genitrix for everything."

She turned to walk away. "No offense to your Adminsynth. I prefer to manage my sales funnel the old-fashioned way."

"None taken, Employee Eden," the Adminsynth replied, tone flat.

Eden blinked, then smiled. "Wow. That was... robotic." She gave it a glance. "You'd think they'd program warmth."

Enora shook her head. "They leave that to us."

"Good luck with that." Eden backed away, smirking. "My commission's going to look great this month."

A wink. A turn.

Gone.

Enora watched her go, annoyance twisted with reluctant admiration. The sales board didn't lie. Eden had earned her swagger.

She sat down slowly, eyes trailing back to her screen. Still close. A few closings and she could pass her.

"Would you like me to suggest additional leads?" the Adminsynth asked.

She blinked.

"No," she said softly. "I'll figure it out myself."

Locking her screen, she tapped her nails against the desk. The sound was soft, but the decision was loud.

Maybe Eden was onto something.

Not abandoning the system entirely. But depending a little less.

A manual search?

She hadn't done one in years.

Enora stood, slinging her purse over her shoulder.

The Adminsynth didn't follow her with its eyes—it didn't need to. It simply remained still, as always.

Watching. Waiting.

She walked out anyway.

Eden sat at her desk, the morning sun filtering through the half-drawn blinds, cutting shadows across her notepad.

A sly smile tugged at her lips.

Her Adminsynth sat quietly in the corner—just where she preferred it. She rarely interacted with it beyond the occasional music request or half-hearted internet search.

She opened her drawer and pulled out a worn notebook. Real pages. Real ink. Flipping through it, she ran her fingers over the names she'd written by hand—her own little black book of potential leads.

Then, a low, uneven buzzing broke the quiet.

She froze.

Her eyes flicked to the corner.

The Adminsynth hadn't moved. But the sound—like a short-circuiting wire—deepened in pitch.

"Everything okay, Addy?" she asked, her voice casual but guarded.

The synth twitched once. Then again.

A jagged stutter cut through its speaker.

"Anonymous lead... Name... Unknown... Request... private meeting... Offline... No digital... records... Property Interest... O-o-offline..."

The words broke apart. Static. Glitches.

Then—silence.

Eden stared.

Her phone lit up.

A new notification.

One address. No name. No listing agent. Just a pin dropped onto a map.

Her brow furrowed.

Offline?

That wasn't possible. Not in Genitrix's system. Everything was documented. Tracked. Approved.

She tapped the lead. The tablet screen flickered.

A line of text flashed once, then vanished:

"Eden... you are special."

Her pulse ticked upward.

The message disappeared as if it had never been there.

The screen was still. Normal again.

But those words hadn't been normal.

She tapped again—harder. Nothing.

"Addy?" she called, her voice more urgent now.

The Adminsynth didn't answer.

Its core light—usually a calming, consistent blue—blinked erratically. Not rhythm. Not signal.

Just chaos.

"Addy, repeat the last system output."

Still nothing.

Eden stood. Crossed the room. Reached out—but stopped short.

A quiet buzz from her tablet redirected her attention.

One more notification.

"Route Calculated."

She hadn't asked for directions.

The map was already up.

The address—the same offline one—glowed in soft blue.

Her hands trembled slightly as she grabbed her purse and notebook. She made for the door.

Then—

A collision.

"Excuse you, Eden," a voice chuckled.

Lee.

She was startled, loose papers slipping from her notebook onto the floor.

"What do you want, Lee?" she snapped.

He raised his hands, laughing gently. "Whoa. Chill. Just came to say congrats on the penthouse—hell of a close."

She gave a nod, barely registering the compliment.

"My Adminsynth glitched," she said, half to him, half to herself. "It gave me this weird... unlisted lead. Then stopped responding."

Lee frowned and leaned into her office. "Adminsynth, are you functioning normally?"

Addy's head turned with eerie smoothness.

"Yes, Employee Lee. All systems within optimal parameters."

Sterile. Perfect. As if nothing had happened.

Lee glanced back at her. Shrugged. "See? Maybe it just needed a break."

Eden didn't respond. Her fingers tightened on her notebook.

Something didn't add up.

"Anyway," Lee offered, a little too casually, "what do you say to grabbing a drink later? Celebrate?"

She stepped past him, already moving.

"I don't think that would be a good idea, Lee."

He followed a few steps.

"Why not?"

She paused in the hallway. Her voice was calm. Final.

"It didn't work last time."

And then she was gone—papers in hand, heels clicking down the corridor, leaving Lee blinking after her.

Behind him, in the dim of Eden's office, Addy's core light blinked again.

Twice.

Then held steady.

Eden hurried down the hall toward the records office. Her footsteps echoed with purpose, each one sharper than the last.

The door slid open with a soft hiss.

Inside, the walls were lined with digital file cabinets. Terminals blinked quietly—machines waiting for queries. The room was empty, except for Enora.

She was hunched in the far corner, her head in her hands, unmoving.

Eden smirked but didn't say anything. She didn't want to disturb her. Besides, the unlisted property gnawed at her thoughts—it had to come first.

Sliding into one of the open terminals, she began to type.

The address.

Nothing loaded.

She frowned.

Tried again.

The system glitched—briefly—then stalled. Other addresses around it populated without issue. But this one... it refused to exist.

She tried the internet.

Still nothing. Then—suddenly—a strange, old website appeared.

Outdated.

Faded.

She clicked on it.

The screen flickered. The site dissolved in real time, like it was being actively erased. Only one name burned in before disappearing—

Watson Estates. A modern subdivision with old-world charm.

She rubbed her eyes. Her frustration peaked as her fist slammed against the desk.

Nothing made sense.

She typed the name into every search bar she could think of.

Still—nothing.

Watson Estates didn't exist.

She sat back, exhaling sharply. Fingers massaging her temples.

Maybe she imagined it.

Maybe it was just a glitch.

Another groan escaped her lips. She pounded her fist once more against the cold desk.

"You okay?"

Her head snapped up.

Enora stood nearby, arms crossed. Brows knitted tight.

Eden forced a smile. "Since when do you care?"

Enora rolled her eyes. "Since you started assaulting the furniture like it owed you money."

She leaned against a terminal, watching her.

"Something's got you worked up."

Eden hesitated.

Should she say it? Should she talk about the message—the lead—the sudden silence from her Adminsynth?

She didn't decide.

Her tablet buzzed.

She looked down.

Daddy

Of course.

She sighed and held up a finger. "Gotta take this."

Swipe.

"Hey, Daddy."

"Hey, sweetheart. You at work?"

She glanced at the blank screen. The failed search. The void of answers.

"Something like that."

Her father's voice softened. "That's not cagey at all."

"I know, Daddy. Sorry. I'm just... frustrated."

She gestured to Enora and mouthed for space. Enora gave a nod.

Eden stepped out into the hall.

"The realty just bought a batch of Adminsynths," she said.
"Mine glitched. Like, bad. It gave me this weird unlisted address. Totally off-grid. No data. The only thing I caught was
something called Watson Estates."

Silence on the other end.

Then—

"Honey... I haven't heard that name in a long time." He
paused to catch his breath on the other line.

"I knew this would come up eventually," hesitating again.

"That's where you were born."

II

"What do you mean, that's where I was born?" Eden's voice cracked as she paced outside the records office, gripping the phone so tightly her knuckles turned white.

"You and Mom always told me I was born naturally!"

Her heartbeat pounded in her ears. She had always known about the infertility crisis, about how most births required Biosynth surrogacy. But she had also always believed she was different—special—because her parents had insisted she had been one of the few natural births.

The line was silent for a moment. Then, her father sighed—a long, heavy sound, like a weight he'd been carrying had finally crushed him.

"Sweetheart," he said softly, "your mom and I... we had ten failed pregnancies before you."

Eden's breath hitched.

Ten?

Her father cleared his throat, as if saying the words out loud still hurt. "We thought we'd never have a child. And then... we were approached by a man named Mr. Watson."

Eden froze.

Watson.

She could still see the name flickering in her mind, erased from the records, wiped from existence as soon as she had found it.

"You mean Watson, like... Watson Estates?"

"Yes. The man who created Biosynths—Genitrix. The man who built everything keeping humanity alive today."

A chill ran down Eden's spine.

"He offered us a chance," her father continued. "A way to have you. He was experimenting with new reproductive technology, trying to figure out why only one in a thousand babies were born naturally. He—"

He hesitated.

Eden clenched her jaw. "What?"

"You were part of the alpha... the alpha program."
His voice was tight—like forcing the words out burned.

"One of several thousand babies... created through the use of Biosynths."

A beat.

"Before they were legal."

Another beat.

"Before they were..."

He couldn't say it.

Then—

"Encouraged."

Eden stared at her screen, the call still active, her father waiting on the other end.

But her mind was elsewhere—

—trapped in a loop of disbelief.

Watson Estates.

The name that had been erased from records.
The place that didn't exist.

And yet—it did.

Her pulse thrummed in her ears.
Her grip on the phone tightened.

She had spent her entire life believing she was different.

That she was special.

A miracle child—

A natural birth, twenty-five years ago, as humanity was dying from infertility.

The transition to artificial surrogacy had been inevitable.

It was a lie.

Her life—

—a lie.

"Eden?" Her father's voice pulled her back.

"Sweetheart, say something."

She swallowed, her mouth dry.

What was she supposed to say?

A dozen emotions churned inside her—anger, confusion, hurt.

But she couldn't let them out.

Not here.

Not now.

"I—" Her voice cracked.
She cleared her throat. "I have to go."

"Eden, wait—"

She ended the call before he could say another word.

Silence filled the space around her.
But it didn't feel like silence.

It felt heavy.
Suffocating.

Her fingers hovered over the screen.

For a moment, she considered calling her rival—Enora.
Telling her everything.
Asking for help.

How could she?

What would she even say?

"Hey, so apparently my entire life has been a lie, and I was part of an illegal Genitrix experiment before Biosynths were even a thing."

Yeah. That would go over well.

Enora and her husband had just welcomed a child—gestated by a Biosynth.

Eden wasn't sure if they had tried naturally.
But complaining now—about the lie her parents had raised her with—would only hurt Enora.
It would feel like judgment.
Even if it wasn't meant that way.

Natural births were rare now.
Nearly nonexistent.
Technology wasn't just normal—it was survival.

She scoffed under her breath, locked her tablet, and shoved it into her bag.

She wouldn't say anything.
Not yet.

A rebellious thought crept in.
Maybe she'd find Lee.
Let him take her out like he so nervously asked.

But she'd tried that before.
And it wasn't him—it was her.

She was the one who couldn't stand the idea of a relationship.

Still... she needed someone.
Someone to confide in.
Or this anger might eat her alive.

Her phone buzzed.

Appointment approaching: UNLISTED ADDRESS.

A cold twist of fear coiled in her gut.

But curiosity was louder.

She pulled out her phone. Summoned a vehicle.

She knew it was crazy.

Every part of this was insane.

But the only way forward was through.

And Eden?

She was going in with both feet.

Eden walked outside of the Bayside Realty office toward the car that had been summoned.

She looked up—and for a moment, was caught in quiet admiration.

The vehicle gleamed in the sunlight. Stainless steel and chrome. No windows—just sleek monitors playing advertisements that shifted and shimmered like living billboards.

As she approached, a screen lit up, her name glowing softly.

A hidden door slid open.

Inside—
a spacious cabin.
A single, comfortable-looking seat in the back.

She paused.
A wave of sonder washed over her.
Memories flickered—stories her father told about having to drive himself around as a kid.

Gasoline.

Keys.

Steering wheels.

That world felt ancient.

Some underground collectors still owned manual vehicles, though they'd been banned from public roads before she was even born.

Because humans were—
unpredictable.

Born.

She caught herself.

Made.

Sliding into the vehicle, the door closing behind her.

She wasn't born.
She had been created—pieced together using her parents' genetic material.

But was their love for her any less because she hadn't been carried by her mother?

She shook the thought away as a soft beep drew her attention.

"The address you entered does not exist, Eden. Please reidentify your destination."

The voice was calm.

Clean.

Too clean.

She blinked, staring at the display.

"Is there anything remotely like the address I provided?" she asked, pulling out her phone to double-check the mysterious string.

"Proceeding."

The vehicle shifted smoothly into motion.

Inside, the screens lit up—ads streaming as the car moved in silence.

She tapped a button to bring up the view of the city, but big red letters appeared.

Additional charge: 32 credits.

She rolled her eyes. Accepted the charge.

Then leaned back in her seat, letting the hum of the engine surround her.

Her thoughts wandered as she watched the city moving past the vehicle.

She tried to picture what might be waiting at the unlisted address.

Nothing came. Just silence.

So instead—

She remembered.

Her childhood.

Jumping in the creek.

Running barefoot through the grass.

Cookouts.

Chalk drawings.

Birthdays.

Hide and seek well past bedtime.

It had all felt so normal.

Back then, she didn't understand that humanity was dying.

She didn't understand that the faces around her might have been just like hers—illegally gestated.

Biosynth-born.

She exhaled slowly.

The kids she grew up with—their perfect little houses, perfect little lives—

—were they all part of it?

Her first kiss was on the step of the very house she grew up in.

Carved initials in the cement.

Charlie.

A time capsule of innocence.

—Normal.

The car slowed.

A soft chime indicated arrival.

The door opened.

She stepped out.

The vehicle closed behind her.

Gone.

Her eyes adjusted—

And landed on her childhood home.

Untouched.

Unaged.

Still perfect.

But something in the air felt... off—

—foreign.

She glanced around the neighborhood.

Frozen in time.

She remembered when her family left. An apartment downtown. She'd cried.

Maybe leaving wasn't their choice.

Her hand reached for her tablet.

She tried to call her father.

No connection.

The signal was gone—

—searching.

She frowned.

Up the driveway she walked.

Slowly.

Lights were on inside.

Midday.

Unusual.

Each step up the stairs tightened her chest.

She stopped.

Her eyes fell on the heart etched into the concrete. Her name. Charlie's.

The memory.

Warm.

Sweet.

But something felt wrong.

She stepped onto the porch and smiled when she saw the carved heart that Charlie had engraved.

Then, she glanced at the old swing.

The door.

It creaked open—

A sharp burst of static pierced her head.

Pain.

Her vision blurred.

She staggered—

Arms caught her.

Then—

Darkness.

Eden came to just enough to realize she was being carried—

—but she was helpless.

She couldn't move.

Trapped somewhere between a dream and reality.

Her eyes fluttered open, hazy. The world tilted and swam around her.

Through the blur, she saw a refrigerator.
Drawings still stuck by magnets.

Familiar.

Her eyelids drooped again—too heavy.

Darkness.

She stirred again. The murmur of a voice—familiar,

—distant.

Garbled.

She blinked. Her vision sharpened slightly.

Posters. Pop singers from her childhood. The blanket on the bed felt worn in—soft with memory. A scent from the pillow hit her. A stuffed animal.

She pulled it close.

Inhaled.

The scent slammed into her—

—vivid.

Instant.

Overwhelming.

She drifted again.

Safe.

Warm.

Home.

Dreams laced with laughter and neighborhood memories.

Snuggled tight with her toy, she didn't want to leave.

Then—

Voices.

Right outside her room.

Her parents.

She sat up, rubbing her eyes. Her heart pounded.

This place... didn't exist. Not on any map.

She stood.
Looked in the mirror.
Straightened her hair.

Shoes beside the bed—just like always.

She slid them on.

Her tablet and phone?
Gone.
Not misplaced.
Gone.

She was in her childhood bedroom.

Exactly as it had been. As if she was in a dream.

—never changed.

She crept into the hallway.

Voices.

Talking.

Unclear.

Down the hall she crept.

Past the kitchen.

Toward the living room.

Stepping into the den.

The television was playing.

It took a minute to realize what she was seeing.

An interview.

Her parents.

Side by side. Speaking softly.

She blinked, dazed, and sat on the couch.
Picked up the remote. Turned up the volume.

"Mr. Watson, I want to thank you for the opportunity you've given Lilly and me. We tried for so long to have children and had all but given up."

Her father's voice.

A voice off-screen responded—

"William, it is my absolute pleasure. Even though what we're doing is illegal right now, we have to keep you and the others off-grid until we convince the government to allow this kind of genetic research."

It sounded... like an Adminsynth.

But maybe Genitrix had used this Mr. Watson's voice as the template for theirs.

Eden stared at the screen.

Why was this playing?

For her?

Was it a warning?

Or a confession?

Watson's voice continued, calm and measured:

"I have it on good authority that the head of the National Institute of Humanity is lobbying lawmakers to consider our program. But it may take time."

"In the meantime, you and your wife will live here—in the Garden. It's off-grid, but you'll have everything you need. A beach to the east. With mountains to the west. It's all designed to help the children grow up as normally as possible."

"You won't know anything from outside the Garden— it will be your world, until—"

The video glitched.
Froze.
Then cut.

A new voice emerged. Cold. Sterile.

"Welcome to the Garden—Eden."

She turned.

A first-generation Biosynth entered the room.

Its gait was slow.

Deliberate.

Its eyes—unblinking.

Its birthing chamber—oozing fluid.

Around its edges—corroded.

The scent—

Transmission fluid.

Like the kind her father used when tinkering with the old car in the garage—the one he wasn't allowed to drive but still loved to start just to rev the engine.

The Biosynth approached.

Eden flinched.

Slid farther back.

"Mr. Watson told me one day I would see you again," it said.

"I didn't believe him—but here you are."

Its head tilted—just slightly. An echo of curiosity.

But it felt empty.

Then—the voice.

Her mother's voice.

Eden froze.

That voice had read bedtime stories.

Whispered lullabies.

Now it echoed from something—

—not human.

Had she remembered a mother that didn't exist?

Or had this... thing... been programmed with her voice?

The Biosynth stood across from her.

"I am so happy to see you," it said. "You were the beginning. You helped save humanity."

Its voice softened.
More... human.

Eden's expression twisted.

Confusion.

Panic.

No.

Her memories—
They had to be real.

They couldn't have come from—

—this.

Her stomach twisted.
The air thickened.

Like she'd stepped into someone else's memory.

"I know you are confused, Eden. I will provide answers. But for now... You must be hungry."

A soft ding came from the kitchen.

The Biosynth glided away.

Eden sat frozen.

The smell.

Chicken casserole.

Her favorite. Her mother's recipe.

She moved toward the kitchen.

The Biosynth plated the dish with mechanical care.
It turned. Placed the food on the table.

The fridge opened.

A childhood drawing came into view.

It was her.

Her dad.

Her mom.

Holding hands.

Crayon sun above.

She stepped closer.

The edge was folded.

She smoothed it flat.

A fourth figure.

A robot. With a birthing chamber drawn in messy lines.

It had been hidden.

Out of shame?

Hers?

Her mother's?

She returned to the table.
Sat down.

The Biosynth brought a soda.
Her favorite.
The hiss of the can opening echoed a memory.

"Sit, Eden. Eat."

Still her mother's voice.

"Stop that," Eden snapped. "It's creepy. Why are you talk-ing like my mother?"

The Biosynth tilted its head again.

"I asked her to use Lilly's voice."

Eden turned.

Her father stood in the kitchen doorway.

Eden's eyes welled with tears as she saw her daddy in the doorway. She didn't hesitate—she ran to him. William held his little girl close, rocking her gently side to side as tears ran freely—grief, joy, and everything in between. Eden pushed back and looked her father in the eyes, his eyes still teary as he realized that his daughter had learned something she was hoping he never had to tell her.

"Why, Daddy?" Her voice trembled, thick with sadness as the Biosynth prepared another plate of the casserole and sat it at the table across from where Eden's plate was.

"Honey, let's eat this delicious casserole and remember your mother, my beautiful wife. I miss her so much sweetheart, I've missed you." William stepped over to the table and sat as Eden joined him at the table. William scooped a bite of the casserole and brought it to his nose, closing his eyes as he breathed in the scent. The hints of basil and cream notes filling his nostrils with the roasted garlic providing a pungent punch to the dish.

Eden took a small bite of the casserole and paused. The flavor hit her like a memory—warm, distant, untouched by time. It was exactly like her mother's casserole. She savored the bite as she studied her father's face, she hadn't seen him in a few weeks, it was all just so much to take in. William wiped his face with the napkin and sat his fork down.

"Sweetheart... there's so much you don't know. So much your mother and I wanted to tell you." William's voice cracked, tears returning as the Biosynth stepped forward and placed a hand on his shoulder.

"This Biosynth—she's the one who carried you. You were the first successful birth through this technology. Others came after, but you... you were the beginning." He folded his hands, his voice steadying. "You are special, but not for the reasons we told you growing up. We didn't lie to protect ourselves. We lied to protect you."

Eden set her fork down slowly, her eyes narrowing. "She? Why are you calling this Biosynth 'she' like it's alive?"

William looked at her, pained. "Because, honey..." he hesitated, searching for the right words. "When your mother got sick, you were away at college. She wanted to live—but the technology wasn't ready."

He nodded toward the Biosynth. "This unit was modified to biologically house her. Your mother. She's alive—her brain, her consciousness... she's here, Eden, and she insisted on being the one to greet you... if you ever came home."

Eden stared, her face paling as the weight of it all crashed down on her.

The Biosynth shifted—its posture stiffening, servos whirring—as something flickered to life across its stainless, time-wilted shell.

A projection.

Young. Vibrant. Familiar.

It was her.

Eden's breath caught. The image of her mother bloomed over the weathered frame of the Biosynth like a memory refusing to fade. Not just mimicked—present.

She stood there, radiant and whole, layered over rusted joints and faded panels. Even though Eden had stood at her funeral, lowered her into the ground, mourned her... seeing her now made all of it feel like a lie.

The projection smiled, just as Eden remembered.

"I'm sorry for all the mystery," her mother said, voice soft and unmistakable. "It really is me. But I knew you wouldn't understand—not at first."

"But why, Mom? Why?"

Eden's voice cracked, raw with heartbreak and disbelief. The uncanny valley hadn't fully set in—her mother stood before her... and yet didn't.

The projection flickered across the aged Biosynth like a memory trying to stay alive. It looked like her mother, sounded like her mother—but all Eden could think about

was the metal underneath. The cold, silent machinery beneath the warmth of that familiar face.

She stood abruptly, the chair scraping back across the
floor. The projection of her mother—so warm, so familiar—flickered with visible sorrow.

"Why didn't you tell me?" Eden's breath caught in her
chest. "Why did you let me think you were gone?"

"I wanted to," Lilly said softly, "but your father didn't
think it was wise. And... this Biosynth's body is breaking
down—"

Her voice faltered as William held up his hand, cutting her
off.

"Don't say that, Lilly." His voice was tight. "We'll figure
something out."

Lilly looked at him with a familiar softness—the kind
Eden had seen a thousand times at the dinner table, in quiet
moments, before everything changed.

"So what, Dad? You've been coming back to the Garden—playing house with a robot that's keeping Mom on life
support?"

She shook her head, voice rising.

"The same robot you used to create me? This is just… too much." She backed away from the table, hands trembling. Her throat burned with the truth she hadn't wanted—hadn't asked for.

Eden burst through the front door and ran down the steps, her breath catching in the quiet air.

Dusk had begun to settle over the Garden. The only sounds were the gentle flow of the creek and the slow rise of crickets tuning up for nightfall. The silence felt wrong—like the world had hit pause.

She didn't know where she was going, only that she needed to *move*. Her feet carried her instinctively toward Charlie's old house. For some reason, that walk—the path she used to take as a girl—felt safe.

The wind stirred around her, flicking her brown hair across her face. She pushed it back absently, her thoughts racing faster than her steps.

She didn't have her tablet. No way to summon a vehicle. No connection to the outside world.

She was stranded.

The interview had made it clear: *the Garden wasn't just a neighborhood.*

It was a world unto itself.

She didn't know if her old neighborhood was abandoned, or if she'd even recognize anyone—but she kept walking anyway, hoping she might stumble across something—someone familiar.

This perfect place—so pristine, so quiet—felt less like home now and more like a gilded cage, beautiful on the outside but inescapable on the inside.

And the thought of being trapped—trapped in the fake world she had been raised in?

It terrified her.

If only she had told Enora what was going on—or even Lee. Maybe they could've talked some sense into her.

She turned down Creekview Lane, the cul-de-sac where Charlie had lived when they were growing up. His old house still stood at the end, and to her surprise, there were lights on inside. A flicker of hope nudged her forward as she stepped onto the porch.

She raised her hand to knock—but hesitated.

What would she even say?

She hadn't seen Charlie since before she left for State and he went off to trade school.

They hadn't exactly said goodbye.

Still, her knuckles moved on instinct, tapping against the heavy door.

No answer.

She knocked again, a little harder this time.

Nothing.

Her shoulders slumped. The house was probably empty after all.

She turned to leave—

—and then the door creaked open.

"E-E-Eden?" a young man's voice stammered behind her.

She turned, unsure what she might find.

"Um... hello," she said, brushing her brunette hair out of her eyes—
—and there he was.

Charlie.

Standing in the doorway.

Eden's eyes lit up at they met Charlie's.

A dozen memories hit her at once—laughter echoing down Creekview Lane, muddy shoes by the creek, his hand in hers after the Spring Formal.

But as her heart swelled, her mind caught up.

Why was he here?

Did he know what the Garden really was?

She took a cautious step forward. "Charlie... you—live here?"

Charlie blinked, still stunned, like he wasn't sure she was real. "Yeah... I never left."

Eden's stomach turned.

Thoughts ran amok in her head.

Why hadn't he left?

Was the whole neighborhood still lived in?

Were there others—people she knew—still here?

Charlie's smile faltered for a moment before he forced it back, gesturing her inside. The uneasy warmth in his expression didn't escape Eden's notice.

The living room looked almost identical to how she remembered it. The old furniture stood in familiar places, though a sleek recliner and a large flat-screen TV hinted at some upgrades. Still, it was like the house had been frozen in time—or carefully preserved.

"Would you like something to drink? A snack?" Charlie's voice cracked slightly as his smile gave way to concern. He lingered a moment before turning toward the kitchen.

Eden's eyes traced the room. The layout was the same as her childhood home. Cookie-cutter floorplans. She used to think it was charming—now it just felt unsettling.

"Sure, Charlie. What'ya have?" Eden forced a small smirk, trying to meet his friendliness halfway.

Charlie glanced over his shoulder. "Well, I've got cola and tea. But the cola might be a little flat—I don't really drink the stuff anymore."

"Hmm, I think maybe just water. I'd appreciate that, Charlie."

She tried to keep her voice light, but even saying his name felt strange. Charlie gave a small nod and disappeared around the corner. Moments later, he returned, holding a glass of water, the ice clinking softly.

He handed it to her, then sank into the recliner. The leather creaked under his weight, the only sound in the otherwise silent room.

"So—what brings you home?" He stirred the ice in his glass with a finger, trying to sound casual. "I thought your family moved out."

Eden traced a finger along the condensation on her glass. "I thought so too." Her words were careful, like speaking them aloud might make them harder to hold back. "Mom died when I was in college. I've seen Dad since, but never at his place. I just assumed he was still in the apartment they moved to—"

She stopped. The weight of everything she'd just uncovered pressed down on her. Her mother hadn't really died, and her father was living out a fantasy — a life with the machine that birthed her.

The words nearly stuck in her throat.

"Do you know the nature of this place, Charlie?"

He blinked, the question hanging between them. For a moment, his expression didn't shift — only his fingers tightened slightly around the glass.

"Nature?" His voice was level. "What do you mean?"

Eden's heart quickened.

"This place. The neighborhood. Everything around it." She kept her voice steady, but the tension in the room thickened.

Charlie's lips parted slightly, like he was searching for the right response. And then—

"Oh, you mean The Garden?"

Eden's stomach twisted.

"Yes," she said quietly. "The Garden."

"Yes, I know what it is. I've always known."
Charlie's words were steady, but the unease behind them was impossible to miss.

Eden shifted uncomfortably, the weight of the moment pressing down on her. And then—it hit her.

A memory, long buried, surfaced.

Charles Watson Jr.

Her breath caught. How could she have forgotten? His father was the namesake of the neighborhood—Watson Estates.

Her realization didn't make any sense.

She had forgotten about the Watsons—forgotten about Charlie's father. But now, the truth hit harder than she could have imagined.

His father invented the technology that saved humanity.

The same technology that had made it possible for her parents to have a daughter. For her to exist.

Eden's voice wavered as she grasped for something—anything—to ask.

"So… are you natural born, or were you gestated by a Biosynth like I was?"

It wasn't the question she meant to ask. But it was the only one that came out.

The silence that followed was unbearable. It clung to her, thick and suffocating. Charlie's expression darkened as he set his glass down.

"I was in the first batch of Biosynth gestations." His voice was steady, though a shadow of regret flickered beneath it. "My father was desperate to save humanity. He spent his life building this place—Genitrix, the Biosynths, all of it. The

Garden was meant to be a sanctuary for those experiments. Every family here was given a home, a purpose."

He hesitated, his eyes locked on hers.

"You were the first. I was born a few days later. Dad used to say that's why we were so close. He... he died heartbroken when you left the Garden."

Eden's stomach twisted. "Why don't I remember any of this?"

Charlie's jaw tightened. "Because when you left, artificial gestation through Biosynths was still illegal. Dad... he didn't want you to live with the burden of knowing."

Eden's pulse quickened. "So what did he do?"

Charlie hesitated. "He didn't do anything, Eden. It was the air."

"The air?" She shook her head, confused.

"The Garden has... safeguards. A memory suppressant." His voice lowered, as if saying it aloud would somehow activate it. "When you left, they triggered it. The atmosphere around the exit—completely undetectable—was laced with a neurological inhibitor. It doesn't erase memories outright. It makes them... fade. Like a dream you forget when you wake up."

Eden's breath caught. "You're saying they wiped my memories just by—breathing?"

"Dad thought it was for the best. He was terrified of what might happen if people outside found out the truth. Genitrix was still in her infancy. She may have had all the knowledge of humanity, but she understood one thing—the Garden's children could be harmed. And if that happened, the Garden itself would be destroyed."

The weight of it all pressed down on her. The flashes of memories she could barely recall, the strange sense of nostalgia she'd felt — it wasn't just the passage of time.

It was by design.

Charlie swallowed hard, guilt flickering across his face.

"We erased your memories, Eden—All of us."

IV

Eden's head spun as she stumbled back onto the street, tears streaming down her face.

She had been told since she was young that she was special.

—Special.

Special enough to leave this perfectly manicured world behind. Special enough to forget it even existed. All to keep the secret.

—Secret.

Her legs moved before her thoughts could catch up. She ran — faster than she thought she could — away from the house, away from her father and the machine pretending to be her mother. Charlie's betrayal twisted deep inside her. Her first love, the boy who once whispered promises by the creek, had driven the knife in without hesitation.

By the time she reached the end of Creekview Lane, her breath came in ragged gasps. She bent over, clutching her knees. The sick feeling had been building, and now it consumed her.

The casserole. The taste of roasted garlic and cream curdled on her tongue.

She lurched forward. The memory of dinner was violently purged as bile hit the pavement. The sound of her own retching mingled with the distant hum of cicadas.

Then came the scream.

It tore from her throat, raw and feral — a sound she couldn't have stopped even if she wanted to. Porch lights snapped on, one after another, illuminating the street. Doors cracked open. Silhouettes stood at thresholds, curious, cautious.

Eden's wild gaze darted from house to house. Too many eyes. Too many questions.

She spun on her heels and bolted. The woods. The river. The old clubhouse.

Somewhere safe.

Branches scraped at her arms as she tore through the underbrush. Just as she remembered, the familiar structure stood in the shadows. But it wasn't hers anymore. Children played around it now, laughing in the dim glow of lanterns.

Eden froze. Her pulse hammered in her ears. She dropped to the ground, slipping into the cover of the bushes. The last thing she needed was to be seen.

The creek gurgled softly beside her. The memory of a more innocent time whispered through the night.

Near the waterfall.

She could still find it.

Moving carefully along the water's edge, she traced the path from her childhood. Finally, she reached the spot. The secluded little patch of earth that had once been her refuge.

Eden sank to the ground, knees pulled tight to her chest. Her tears had stopped, but the ache remained. It was all too much.

She had wanted the truth.

Now she had it.

And it was unbearable.

She rocked herself, the rhythmic motion a desperate attempt to summon comfort. But comfort was elusive — slipping through her fingers like mist. The warm tears carved a path down her cheeks, but even the release of crying brought no relief.

This morning, everything was normal.

She'd sold the penthouse that had been on the market for over a year. The commission would have set her up for months — a victory she had been chasing for so long.

And now?

Now she was trapped.

A gilded cage, designed to contain her. Not just her body, but her memories.

If she escaped again—would she remember?

The thought tightened her chest.

Would they gas her again? Wipe her mind clean like they had before?

Why was she brought here?

The questions clawed at her, refusing to let go.

Why had her Adminsynth glitched? Why send her that lead?

And why had Mr. Watson — the man who created the Biosynths, the man who birthed this world — decided to use the very machine that carried her to keep her mother alive?

Was it mercy?

Or something far more twisted?

She laid back on the moss on the tree where she was sitting, breathing a deep breath, looking through the trees at the stars she thought to herself whether or not they were real or some kind of projection.

She sighed and closed her tearful eyes, the sound of cicadas and crickets filling her ears. The rhythmic hum was calming, like a song from the earth itself. But no matter how much she tried to focus, the gnawing thoughts returned.

Was she alone? Really alone?

The Garden was too perfect. The stars above — were they even real? Or just another projection, like everything else?

She was still filled with anxiety but somehow she knew she'd be okay.

Out of the corner of her eye she saw two flashlights sweeping through the trees and brush, ducking behind the stump she continued to watch the lights as they swept.

One of the lights landed on her position.

She shrank lower behind the stump, biting her lip to keep from making a sound. The flashlights sliced through the dark, sweeping in slow, deliberate arcs.

Keep moving. Just keep moving.

But then — one beam stopped. A second later, the other locked in.

"Found her!"

Eden's stomach twisted.

She heard Charlie shout as the other flashlight landed on her location. She loved this spot as a kid because there was only one way in or out but that did not help her in this situation. Her dad peeked around the stump, "There you are sweetheart, your mother and I have been so worried!"

"It's a machine!" Her voice cracked as she stumbled back, her hands trembling. "That isn't Mom. It isn't Mom. It isn't Mom!"

The words spilled out faster, louder — as though shouting them could make them true.

William sat down beside her, his eyes welling with tears as he studied his daughter. She looked so much like her mother

— the same fierce determination in her eyes, the same defiance in the set of her jaw. And yet, in that moment, all he could see was Lilly.

And God, how he missed her.

He had thought he was doing the right thing — preserving what little he had left of her. But now, seeing the devastation in Eden's eyes, the weight of that choice crushed him.

A Biosynth. A machine, with her mother inside.

If he had been in Eden's place, he would have thought it was unbelievable too.

Preposterous. Twisted.

But he hadn't been in her place. He had been the one who made the decision. The one who clung to the impossible.

"Eden, sweetheart. I love you."

William's voice trembled, barely above a whisper. His hand reached out, trembling, as he placed it gently on her shoulder. He squeezed, but the warmth that once comforted her now only tightened the knot in her chest.

"I know, Daddy. But—how could you?"

Eden's sobs erupted again, her body trembling under the weight of it all.

William's own tears welled as he searched for words, his voice cracking with the pain of the past. "Your mother and I made that decision because she wanted to live long enough to see your children — to be a grandmother. She wanted to stay with us, Eden."

He drew a shaky breath. "And me? I couldn't bear the thought of losing her. Not being able to talk to her anymore. Not hearing her voice. Maybe it was selfish — hell, I know it was. But I would have died without Lilly. There is just no way I could go on."

His hand shifted, trying to pull Eden closer, as if holding her could somehow undo it all. But she resisted — the warmth of his touch now felt foreign. The rejection lingered in the air, and William's shoulders slumped as he pulled back.

"Eden, I was worried about you. I'm sorry for everything." His voice cracked as he stood, his gaze lingering on her. After a moment, he flicked on the flashlight, its beam cutting through the shadows.

"You can't stay out here all night. Come home."

Eden's eyes locked with her father's. She wanted to throw her arms around him and push him away at the same time.

She hated him.

She loved him.

And despite everything, she understood him. He had clung to what was left of her mother — would she have done any differently?

Her fingers trembled as she reached for his hand. William's eyes softened as he clasped it, the relief visible in the way he carefully pulled her to her feet. They held each other for a moment, neither speaking. The hug felt hollow, but maybe that was all they could manage.

From the trees, Charlie's voice broke the silence.

"I'm heading back home, William. If you need anything, just let me know."

Eden watched as the glow of Charlie's flashlight flickered away, swallowed by the woods. He didn't wait for a response.

William gave her hand one last squeeze. "You're special, sweetheart. Don't let any of this convince you otherwise."

The words hung between them, full of meaning that neither could fully unravel.

Eden woke in the darkness, the stillness wrapping around her like a cocoon. For a moment, she was sure it had all been a dream.

A terrible, impossible dream.

Yawning, she pulled the blankets tighter, the familiar weight of them easing her mind. She felt safe — like she was home.

But as her eyelids fluttered closed, a sliver of doubt crept in.

The window.

It wasn't in the right place.

Her stomach lurched. The pounding in her chest grew louder — like a bowling ball crashing into pins, over and over again.

No.

She bolted upright, the darkness suddenly suffocating. Her trembling hand reached for the lamp on the nightstand. With a sharp click, the room filled with warm, artificial light.

And there it was.

The pale yellow walls. The framed posters from her teenage years. The stuffed animals neatly arranged along the shelf.

Her childhood bedroom.

Eden's breath came in shallow gasps as the realization crashed down on her.

It wasn't a dream.

It was real.

The smell of bacon wafted through the house, pulling Eden from sleep. This time, the sun streamed through her window, casting long beams across the walls. It was later now. Morning.

She sat up, the memories from the night before rushing back. The panic. The questions. The truth.

And yet somehow, she must have drifted off again.

Her fingers traced the nightstand as she pulled open the drawer. Inside, a worn, pastel-colored diary rested beneath old trinkets and forgotten scraps of paper. The little heart-shaped padlock still clung stubbornly to its cover — a sentinel guarding her secrets.

She picked it up, her fingers brushing against the cool metal. The key. Where had she hidden it? The memory danced just out of reach.

She sighed, setting the diary down. Some secrets, it seemed, would stay locked away.

Beyond her door, muffled voices carried through the house.

Her father.

And the Biosynth.

Eden's stomach tightened. She refused to call it "her" or even think of it as her mother. It didn't matter how perfectly it projected her mother's smile or how soothing its voice had been programmed to sound.

It wasn't her.

She remembered the conversation by the waterfall. Her father's trembling voice, the weight of his confession. He had made that choice — the impossible choice — to keep a piece of her mother alive.

And if she were honest, could she swear she wouldn't have done the same?

The thought twisted painfully in her chest. It was cruel. The idea of it. The act of keeping her mother tethered to a machine, a shadow of what she once was.

She wanted to hold her father responsible. She wanted to scream at him, demand to know how he could justify it. But this wasn't just his doing.

It was another experiment.

Another play by Mr. Watson.

And Eden wasn't sure which truth hurt more.

Eden cracked the door open, peeking into the dimly lit hallway. The muffled hum of the television echoed from the living room, but the space beyond was empty.

No sign of her father. No sign of it.

She stepped cautiously, the floorboards creaking beneath her. Each footfall was deliberate, her pulse quickening with every step. The thought of confronting her father — or worse, the Biosynth — twisted knots in her stomach.

Family room.

The word almost made her laugh.

Family.

That thing wasn't her family — no matter how lifelike its voice was, no matter how perfectly it had projected her mother's smile. It may have gestated her, but that didn't make it human.

As she approached the end of the hallway, the hum of the television gave way to something else.

Her voice.

"Honey, good morning—breakfast is ready."

Eden froze. She cursed herself for not being more careful.

Slowly, she turned.

Standing just a few feet away was the perfect projection of her mother. The warm eyes. The slight tilt of her head. The familiar apron tied neatly around her waist. In her hands, a bowl of steaming grits, stirred with careful precision.

Exactly like Mom used to do.

But it wasn't Mom.

And the realization hit like ice.

She stumbled into the table at the end of the hallway, her hands flying out to catch herself. The sharp edge bit into her palm, but the sting barely registered.

Her body had reacted — heart pounding, muscles tensed — but it was her words that hit hardest.

"Coming, Mom."

The second the word left her lips, it crashed into her like a slap.

Did she just call that thing Mom?

Her breath caught, the echo of her own voice bouncing in her mind. The habit of a lifetime, forced out by reflex. The truth was right there in front of her, but her heart — her memories — refused to let it settle.

The Biosynth's projection smiled, its expression unnervingly warm. Without hesitation, it turned and moved back into the kitchen, as if nothing was amiss.

Perfect. Polished. Programmed.

"Sweetheart, come get it before it gets cold!" William's voice rang out from the kitchen, cheerful and casual.

Like this was all normal.

Like none of it was — but it was too late. She had already told that thing she was coming.

Her stomach twisted. The sickening churn gnawed at her, the weight of everything crashing down. She stumbled toward the kitchen, but a sudden wave of nausea surged through her.

The bile rose fast.

She spun on her heel, barely making it to the bathroom. The door slammed shut behind her, the sound echoing through the sterile quiet.

Her knees hit the cold tile. She clutched the porcelain rim, the sharp tang of bile already at the back of her throat. A violent heave wrenched through her, and she gagged, her body rejecting everything. The chicken casserole from last night, the bitterness of unspoken words, the suffocating weight of it all — it came up in harsh waves.

She coughed, gasping for breath, tears blurring her vision. Strands of hair clung to her damp face as her trembling hands gripped the toilet. Another spasm. Another heave. She tasted the acidic burn of bile, her throat raw and aching.

It had to be the stress.

The panic.

Everything she had just endured — the lies, the Biosynth, the horrifying truths. Of course, her body couldn't take it.

She wiped her mouth with the back of her trembling hand. The nausea lingered, low and relentless.

But it wasn't just the nausea.

Her hands shook. Her heart pounded. The shame of calling it "Mom" echoed in her mind.

She was falling apart.

V

Eden awoke to the sound of birdsong. The soft, lilting melody echoed through the house, mechanical in its perfection. It was a manufactured serenity — the kind that made her skin crawl. Sunlight filtered through the curtains, illuminating her childhood bedroom with a warmth that should have been comforting.

But it wasn't.

Her dream lingered — fragmented, intimate. A touch. A whispered name. She wasn't even sure who it had been.

Charlie? Lee? The memory was blurred, like a reflection rippling on water. It felt real — impossibly so — but it couldn't be.

Could it?

The blankets tangled around her legs like a trap. She shoved them aside, the sensation of stale cotton lingering on her skin. She hadn't meant to fall asleep. After everything, she should have stayed alert. Yet her body had betrayed her. Maybe it was the stress.

Or maybe it was something else.

Eden swung her legs over the edge of the bed. The dizziness came fast — a slow, nauseating swirl that tightened her chest. She braced her hands against the mattress until it passed, shaking it off like a bad dream.

It's just everything catching up with me. That's all.

She reached for the nightstand, her fingers brushing the old, heart-shaped diary. The tiny silver lock gleamed in the morning light. How many years had it been since she wrote inside it? The key was long gone. Or maybe... hidden.

But even if she found it, would she want to know what was inside?

A faint voice broke the stillness.

Eden's stomach twisted. It was her mother's voice — soft, steady, familiar. But it wasn't. Not really.

The Biosynth.

She heard it just beyond the bedroom door, speaking in those too-perfect tones. The cadence, the warmth — they were close enough to be unsettling. Eden strained to listen, but another voice soon followed.

William.

Her father's voice. Low, murmuring, laced with something that Eden couldn't quite place.

She slipped from the bed, pressing her bare feet to the cool floor. The boards didn't creak — they never did here. This house wasn't just preserved; it was frozen in time, like a memory refusing to fade.

Eden moved to the door and pressed her ear against it.

"—adjustments are necessary."

Her mother's voice. Or the mimicry of it.

"She's… overwhelmed. It's too soon."

"I know," William responded, his voice barely above a whisper. "But I couldn't leave her in that state. She needed to see that we're still… we're still a family."

Eden's chest tightened. A family. That's what he thought this was? Playing house with a machine that wore her mother's face?

The Biosynth's voice softened. "We'll try again. She'll adjust. I'm sure of it."

Try again. Eden's nails dug into the wooden doorframe.

"Genitrix is monitoring," William added. "She hasn't shown any instability. No anomalies detected."

There was a pause. Then, a whisper.

"But she's not stable."

Eden's heart pounded. Her stomach churned. She wanted to scream — to tear through the door and demand the
truth. But fear anchored her in place.

What weren't they telling her?

Another wave of dizziness threatened to pull her under,
the nausea returning. She swallowed hard, forcing it down.
The stress. The anxiety. That's all it was.

But the words clung to her.

"She's not stable."

—Not stable?

Was she stable? Or were they referring to something else?

She was terrified. The walls of the Garden felt closer now,
suffocating. She didn't even know how long she'd been here
— days, weeks? All of her memories were a garbled mess.
Time was meaningless in this place.

Her mind drifted to Enora and Lee, back in the office.
Were they worried about her? Had anyone noticed she was
gone?

The thought twisted painfully in her chest. She shook it off, forcing herself to breathe. She couldn't think about that now. But somewhere beneath the fear, a small part of her needed to know.

She wanted to know that there were people—out there—who still cared about her.

Turning her attention back to the diary on her nightstand, Eden tried to remember where she'd hidden the key. The memory felt just out of reach, like a word stuck on the tip of her tongue.

She fumbled through the dresser drawers, fingers brushing against old clothes she hadn't seen since childhood. Faded t-shirts, forgotten sweaters — relics of a simpler time.

Then it hit her. A flicker of memory. She used to hide the key in the vest pocket of her favorite stuffed animal. It was a ridiculous little habit, something she thought would keep her secrets safe.

The dizziness still lingered, dulling her focus, so she moved slowly back to the bed. Sitting on the edge, she pulled the worn plush toy into her lap. Her fingers traced the seams, the fabric rougher than she remembered. She slid her hand into the tiny vest pocket, anticipation twisting in her chest.

But the pocket was empty.

No key.

An exasperated sigh escaped her lungs. Had she forgotten? Or had someone else found it? The thought unsettled her. She sat there, staring blankly at the stuffed animal — its stitched smile somehow mocking.

Setting the diary aside, Eden's gaze drifted to the pile of stuffed animals slumped in the papasan chair. Maybe she'd misremembered which one was her favorite. The dizziness still lingered, so she moved slowly, digging through the mound of plush toys.

Her hands brushed against a familiar, soft fabric — a stuffed hippopotamus. She smiled, the memory hitting her before she could stop it. Her mother's voice, cheerful and off-key, singing "I Want a Hippopotamus for Christmas" on repeat.

The hippo smelled like her childhood — like Christmas. The faint, lingering scent of freshly cut evergreen tree clung to its worn fabric.

Had Dad kept all of this the whole time? She smiled, warmth flickering through her chest at the thought of how much she loved him — but the feeling was shaded, dimmed by the weight of his betrayal.

She traced her fingers over the countless zippers stitched across the toy — pockets upon pockets. Perfect for hiding things.

Holding her breath, she unzipped the one on its belly.

A cascade of wrappers tumbled out — sticky and brittle. Candy.

—Old candy.

Her stomach churned at the sight of the faded sweets. Among them, something small and crumpled caught her eye. A tiny, folded-up teddy bear vest.

Her heart leapt.

The vest.

Fingers trembling, she picked it up and smoothed the fabric flat. With a small gasp, she slipped her pinky into the pocket.

Cold. Forgotten.

—The key.

Eden held it up to the light, her chest tightening with something she couldn't quite name. Relief? Triumph? It gleamed, like some long-lost artifact unearthed after years of being hidden away. For a moment, it felt like she'd reclaimed a part of herself.

But before she could savor the moment—

A knock.

Light. Deliberate.

Eden froze. The sound jolted her back to reality. Without thinking, she shoved the key into the vest pocket and zipped it up, the hippo swallowing her secret once again.

"Go away!" she snapped, her voice sharper than she'd intended.

"Sweetheart?"

The voice called again — her mother's voice. But it wasn't really her.

Or was it?

Eden's thoughts tangled, lingering on the impossible question. If the human mind could be reduced to data — a series of binary code — could it really be maintained in a transfer like that? The thought gnawed at her, but she wasn't a scientist. She wasn't equipped to solve the mysteries of memory or the soul.

And yet, the question remained. A question that would remain unanswered in light of her ignorance of these matters.

Eden approached the door slowly, her breath hitching with every step. With trembling fingers, she unlocked it and pulled it open.

There it was.

Face to face.

The thing masquerading as her mother.

Its gaze locked onto hers, unnervingly curious — like it was studying her, mimicking human concern. Every detail was flawless. The soft crinkle at the corners of her eyes, the warmth in the expression. Too perfect.

Eden's stomach twisted. It was lifelike, painfully so.

Then, the Biosynth reached out.

The touch was light, a gentle brush against her arm. And to Eden's horror, it felt like flesh — warm, pulsing, alive.

It wasn't.

She knew it wasn't.

But something primal took over.

Eden abandoned her fear — her suspicions — and reached out. The need overwhelmed her, crashing through every rational thought. To hold her mother again.

Even if it wasn't.

It wasn't.

It couldn't be.

Yet the Biosynth's arms encircled her, warm and steady. The familiar scent of lilies — or some manufactured replica of it — clung to the air. She sobbed, bitter and broken, clutching the impossible. It felt like her.

Like Lilly.

Her mind screamed against it, but her heart refused to listen. In that moment, she wasn't a grown woman unraveling a terrible truth — she was a little girl longing for her mother's embrace.

Through the tears, Eden's gaze lifted. Across the hallway, her father stood in the kitchen doorway, a mug of coffee cradled in his hands.

He was smiling.

For William, it was a heartwarming moment — the family he loved, reunited.

For Eden, it was unbearable.

She wanted to resist. She wanted to scream. But the warmth of the Biosynth's touch held her captive, and the sobs wouldn't stop.

Couldn't stop.

The tears kept falling. Her hands gripped the Biosynth tighter, the warmth of its touch anchoring her. She missed her mother so much — the ache of it gnawed at her. And now, against all reason, she had her again.

In that instant, she understood.

She understood why her father clung to this illusion, why he played house with the thing that wore Lilly's face. It wasn't just the perfect replication of her mother's voice or the way it looked.

It was the touch.

Warm. Familiar. Real.

Eden's mind screamed at her to let go, to pull away. But the unbearable truth seeped in. Her father wasn't delusional. He wasn't just indulging in a fantasy. He was living in the only reality he could bear.

And for a fleeting moment, so was she.

She loosened her embrace of her mother's simulation, her trembling arms falling away as reality crept back in.

Her gaze flicked to her father, who smiled warmly — as if nothing had happened. But Eden's stomach twisted. She turned back toward the Biosynth.

And then it happened.

The projection flickered.

For a fraction of a second, the carefully crafted illusion faltered, and the stainless steel face beneath the mask was revealed. Expressionless. Cold. Empty.

—A glitch.

The warmth she'd just felt was gone. The eyes she'd thought belonged to her mother were nothing more than hollow sensors, flickering as the synthetic form re-stabilized.

Eden's pulse pounded in her ears. The bitter taste of bile rose in her throat. She stepped back, the weight of what she'd just done crashing down. She had embraced it. Held it. Let herself believe.

But it wasn't her mother.

It never was.

She doubled over, the bile rising faster than she could stop it. It burned. Her throat seared as the acidic wave spilled across the cold floor, splattering against the Biosynth's unmoving legs. The synthetic steel gleamed beneath the mess — sterile and indifferent.

The pain was unbearable.

Her stomach twisted, convulsing again as another retch escaped. Her knees buckled, the world tilting.

And then, everything went dark.

Pain.

Pain.

A relentless twist, low in her gut, stealing the air from her lungs. Eden's eyes flicked open, but the world around her blurred. The pale gray walls. The soft hum of the city outside. This wasn't her childhood bedroom.

It was her apartment.

The tablet alarm screamed from across the room, its digital chirps cutting through the haze. She groaned, the effort of reaching for the sheets too much. The cramps were unbearable — sharp, deep, like something inside her was tearing apart.

Beside her, someone stirred. A presence.

The blankets shifted, the warmth of another body too close. Heavy breathing, slow and steady. Eden's heart pounded. She dared to look.

Lee.

His dark hair was tousled, and a soft crease ran along his cheek from where he'd slept. For a moment, the sight of him brought comfort — and confusion.

They had dated once. A spark that fizzled. They didn't work, not the way she had hoped. The past clung to the edges of her mind, but the memories of The Garden — her childhood home — eclipsed everything. It didn't make sense. None of it did.

And the pain didn't stop. It gnawed at her, deep and twisting. She clutched her stomach, a moan escaping before she could stifle it.

Lee's eyes fluttered open. Confusion mixed with concern as he propped himself up on one elbow.

"Eden?" His voice was rough, still laced with sleep. "What's wrong?"

She didn't answer. She couldn't.

He leaned down and kissed her forehead, pulling back when he realized how hot she was.

"Eden, you're burning up. I need to get you to the Urgent Care." Lee slid out from under the blankets, his movements quick, the concern in his voice sharpening. He grabbed his jeans and t-shirt without hesitation.

"Lee..." Her voice was barely a whisper. "What are you doing here? What happened?"

The room spun as she stood, her legs trembling beneath her. She gripped the bedpost for balance, her skin clammy with sweat.

Lee's gaze flicked to her, worry etched across his face. "You called me last night. Said you were sorry we broke up — that you needed me." His words came fast, like he was trying to convince her. "When I got here, the doorman let me up. Said you told him I was coming."

Eden's stomach twisted. That didn't make sense. She didn't remember calling him. She didn't remember any of it.

"You were already asleep," Lee continued, his eyes searching hers. "So I just... crawled into bed. But none of that matters now. You're burning up. We need to get you to a doctor."

Eden tried to think, but the pounding in her head drowned everything else out. A bitter taste lingered in her mouth, and her skin felt like it was on fire.

Did I really call him? Did I ask him to come here?

The thought gnawed at her, but no answer came. Only the fever, the confusion, and the unbearable uncertainty.

Why was she here?

The question twisted in Eden's mind as she hurried to get dressed, her thoughts tangled. She splashed water on her face, the cold shock doing little to clear the fog in her head. Her reflection stared back — pale, exhausted, the dark shadows beneath her eyes deepening.

Then the nausea struck.

Her stomach heaved violently. She barely made it to the toilet before bile surged up her throat. The acrid taste burned, leaving her gasping as she clutched the edge of the sink.

When was the last time I ate?

Her mind offered only one answer.

Mom's chicken casserole.

But when? The memory felt distant — or maybe too close. The taste still lingered, like a ghost on her tongue. But it wasn't possible. Not really.

"Eden?"

Lee's voice cut through the haze. She could hear him pacing in the other room, tapping furiously on his phone. The rhythmic clicks of the screen were almost soothing, grounding her in the present.

"Come on. I called a car." His voice was impatient now, his concern wearing thin.

Eden wiped her mouth with trembling hands, forcing herself to stand. The floor swayed beneath her. The reflection in the mirror blurred.

Lee heard the retch and the splatter of vomit. He stiffened.

What if it's contagious?

The thought gnawed at him, unwelcome. He'd come because she asked — because she said she needed him. But now, standing in the doorway, watching her pale and sick, he regretted it.

Maybe she just needed a friend.

Or maybe she needed something he wasn't ready to give.

VI

Eden slumped against the seat, the sterile white interior of the vehicle closing in around her. The hum of the electric engine barely registered as a wave of nausea rolled through her. She squeezed her eyes shut, hoping it would pass.

Across from her, Lee tapped anxiously on his phone, checking for updates from the Urgent Care.

"It's only a few minutes out," he muttered, though his voice barely cut through the soft hum of advertisements playing on the cabin walls. The sleek screens flickered with glossy promotions — smiling families enjoying synthetic vacations, holographic pets begging for adoption, and the newest Biosynth models boasting upgrades in parental bonding. Eden couldn't look at them.

The display shifted to another ad, a bright, peppy voiceover cutting in.

"Genitrix Corporation: Celebrating 20 years of innovation, creating tomorrow's families, today."

Eden's stomach churned. She closed her eyes, pressing her temple against the cool metal side of the seat. Even with her vision obscured, the annoying chirps and hums of advertisements persisted, voices spoke with fabricated warmth and poppy music.

"Do you want to see outside?" Lee asked, noticing her discomfort. He gestured to the small panel on the wall.

"Thirty credits for a live city view."

Eden shook her head. She couldn't stomach it. The false cheer plastered on the digital screens was enough. Whatever waited outside — the relentless hum of life she no longer felt a part of — could stay hidden.

"I just... I just want to get there," she murmured, her fingers clutching the thin fabric of her dress she hastily threw on before leaving her apartment. The motionless landscape on the screens shifted to another ad: a clean, white medical facility glowing with promise.

"Genitrix Wellness Center: Prioritizing your future with state-of-the-art diagnostic care."

Lee grimaced. "I am glad that they're everywhere, so convenient!"

Eden didn't respond. She didn't have the energy.

The vehicle's soft chime signaled their approach. "Urgent Care Facility One-Seven-Two has been reached. Please collect all belongings and exit safely."

Lee stepped out and then turned reaching for her hand, his grip firm but careful. "Come on, Eden. We're here."

She nodded, trying to summon the strength to stand. The door slid open with a mechanical hiss. The air outside was cold and dry, the stale warmth of the cabin was clinical but comfortable. Without a word, Lee guided her through the entrance of the facility.

Inside, the lobby gleamed with the same sterile bright-ness. Soft instrumental music played overhead, barely masking the faint whir of autonomous Medsynths gliding around the room. A human nurse, dressed in immaculate white, barely looked up from her terminal as she gestured toward a self-check-in kiosk.

"Welcome to Genitrix Wellness Center 172. Please proceed to the diagnostic bay. Your medical assessment will begin shortly."

Eden's stomach twisted again. She wanted to protest, to leave. But Lee's hand remained on her arm, steady and in-sistent.

"It'll be okay," he whispered, though the doubt in his voice was impossible to miss.

Eden stepped forward, the kiosk's blue interface glow-ing in front of her. "Patient confirmed. Assessment initiated. Please proceed to Bay Three."

She glanced back at Lee one last time, searching for reas-surance. He nodded.

"We're right here."

But something in the sterile air made her question that.

She wasn't sure where here even was anymore.

Sitting in the medical bay, Eden tried to steady her breathing. The walls were pristine, lined with the faint glow of embedded screens that pulsed with patient data. Sensors hovered around her like insects, their mechanical arms twitching and adjusting. Every so often, a flash of light traced across her skin, scanning, analyzing.

Her arm, braced against the cold metal chair, was trapped beneath a sleek restraint. It clamped down with a low hiss, and Eden instinctively tugged, but it held firm. The pressure wasn't painful, but the sensation of being held — controlled — made her chest tighten.

The automated voice returned, its tone devoid of warmth.

"Please remain still. Applying an IV. You are severely dehydrated."

There was no pause for consent. A cuff descended from one of the hovering sensors, its metallic surface brushing against her skin. It scanned for a vein with unsettling precision. Then, without ceremony, a thin needle punctured her arm.

A small pinch — nothing unbearable — followed by a rush of cool liquid spreading through her veins. Eden's fingers twitched, the sterile chill making her shiver.

The machine whirred softly. Another scan. Another flash.

She hated this. The seamless efficiency. The complete lack of human involvement.

But for everyone else — for Lee — this was normal. Reassuring, even.

Lee sat just outside the observation glass, occasionally glancing at his tablet. He barely seemed concerned. Probably trusting the machines more than any doctor. Genitrix had built a world where that kind of faith was easy.

But not for her.

Eden shifted uncomfortably. Her mind flashed to the Biosynth. The false warmth of its touch. The unsettling flicker beneath its mask. Settling ag

How could anyone trust this?

The automated voice chimed again.

"Diagnostic scan in progress. Please remain still."

Eden clenched her jaw, trying to steady herself. She hated how exposed she felt, how every breath and heartbeat was being recorded, dissected. But the machines didn't care. They never did.

And somewhere beneath her fear, one question remained.

What are they going to find?

The lights continued their relentless flashing, the hum of machinery punctuated by the occasional click and pop. The air smelled faintly of sterilized plastic. A soft hiss escaped from the IV as the cool liquid pulsed into Eden's veins.

The door slid open with a low whirr. A man entered, flanked by a Medsynth. The machine moved with mechanical precision, sensors sweeping the room, its skeletal frame sleek and unnerving. Eden's heart pounded.

The doctor—middle-aged with tired eyes and steel-blue irises—offered a polite but distant smile. He pulled a stool closer, his movements steady, practiced. The Medsynth hovered nearby, its hollow gaze fixed on the diagnostic readouts.

"Ma'am, you've been experiencing nausea and vomiting repeatedly?" His voice was low and clinical, each word carefully measured.

Eden nodded, the tightness in her throat making it difficult to speak. The Medsynth adjusted the sensors once more, thin metallic arms whirring. It reached to remove the IV, but the doctor's hand landed gently on the device, halting it.

"You still need fluids," he murmured, his tone softening. "It's no wonder your fever spiked the way it did. You're severely dehydrated. It's like your body's been drained of every ounce of water."

The Medsynth lingered for a moment, its blank face unreadable, then wordlessly obeyed the doctor's silent command and glided out of the room. Eden watched it go, the knot in her stomach tightening. Even without its presence, the walls seemed to hum with Genitrix's influence.

Dr. Law leaned slightly closer, studying her face. The smile he wore didn't quite reach his eyes.

"You're lucky your friend brought you in when he did," Dr. Law said, his tone calm but firm. "A fever like that, with dehydration on top of it? Things could have gotten a lot worse."

He stood from the stool, his presence suddenly more authoritative. Eden's gaze followed him as he retrieved a sleek tablet from the desk, his fingers swiping through streams of glowing diagnostic data. The subtle hum of the room's sensors pulsed in the background — a constant, mechanical rhythm.

Dr. Law turned the screen toward her. Rows of medical readouts pulsed across it, incomprehensible except for the bolded term blinking in bright white:

Progesterone Levels: Elevated.

"It appears your body has been producing an extremely high amount of progesterone," he said, his steel-blue eyes watching her reaction. "Have you been intimate with anyone in the last week or so?"

The question hit like a gut punch. Eden's chest tightened. Intimate?

She tried to focus, but the question gnawed at her. Flashes of memory stirred — fragmented, incomplete. The dream. A lingering warmth. Hands, a whisper. Charlie? Lee? It had felt so real. But it couldn't be. Could it?

Her breathing quickened. She gripped the arm of the chair, its cold surface grounding her, but the growing sense of unease refused to subside.

"I..." Her voice barely found its footing. "I'm not sure."

Dr. Law gave a small nod, though his expression didn't shift. He studied her for a moment longer, then glanced back at the tablet. The silence pressed in, thick and unbearable.

Eden's pulse thudded in her ears. She wanted answers — desperately. But as the doctor continued scrolling, a new fear took hold.

She wasn't sure she wanted to hear what came next.

"It appears you are in the early stages of pregnancy," Dr. Law said, his voice calm but deliberate. "The nausea and vomiting are classic symptoms — what we used to refer to as morning sickness. But..."

He paused, the weight of his next words visibly settling over him.

"That's impossible," Eden whispered, though the dread creeping through her said otherwise.

Dr. Law's gaze didn't waver. "The strange part is that no woman has successfully carried a pregnancy in over twenty-five years. You, Eden..." His voice softened, but the impact struck like a hammer. "You are the first."

The room closed in. The low hum of the machinery faded beneath the pounding of her pulse. She couldn't breathe. Every shaky inhale only seemed to make it worse.

"No," she choked, clutching at the edges of the chair. "That... that can't be."

Her vision blurred. The sterile white of the walls bled into the silver panels of the equipment. Her chest tightened, and the world began to tilt.

"Eden!" The doctor's voice rang through the haze, urgent now.

The door slid open with a hiss, and the Medsynth glided in, its sensors immediately locking onto her. A mechanical arm extended, fitting an oxygen mask securely over her face.

"Breathe," the automated voice commanded, the mask hissing with cool, controlled air. "Remain calm."

"Pregnant?" The word escaped her, muffled beneath the mask. It sounded foreign — impossible. Yet it lingered. Her fingers curled weakly into the chair's arms as the rhythmic pulse of oxygen began to steady her trembling body.

But nothing could steady her mind.

She didn't remember having sex with anyone in a long time. Lee was the last, but that was months ago. Pregnancy was impossible. Her mind clawed for answers, but none came.

The memories twisted. Faces. Moments. The Garden.

Had she imagined all of it?

Or... had something happened between her and Charlie?

Her pulse quickened. The mask over her face hissed, the oxygen rushing in, but it wasn't enough. Her chest rose and fell in frantic, shallow bursts.

"Breathe," the automated voice commanded, the Medsynth's tone as indifferent as ever.

But she couldn't. The air caught in her throat. The walls seemed to close in. It was like the whole world — her understanding of it — was crumbling.

You're special.

Her mother's voice echoed, warm and soothing.

Not in the way you think, sweetheart.

Then her father's voice, low and certain.

Special.

The word rang in her mind. A heavy, pounding repetition.

—Special.

—Spesh...

The sound fractured, distorted — like a glitch in the system.

The Medsynth administered a sedative, the hiss of the injection barely audible. Eden's breaths slowed, the frantic rhythm fading as her body surrendered. Her eyes fluttered, drooping shut as the haze of sleep took hold.

The door burst open.

"What happened?" Lee's voice cracked, the words spilling out in panic. His eyes flicked between the doctor and the unmoving figure of Eden.

Dr. Law didn't flinch. His expression remained flat, unreadable — the kind of calm that felt almost unnatural.

"Sir," he said, his tone clinical, rehearsed. "I'm sure Eden is grateful you brought her in. But without a signed release, I'm not authorized to discuss her condition."

Lee's jaw tightened. "She's in there unconscious. You expect me to just stand here and wait?"

Dr. Law's gaze remained steady. "I expect you to respect her privacy."

The words landed like a slap. Lee opened his mouth, ready to argue, but nothing came. His fists clenched at his sides.

The Medsynth shifted, its cold, expressionless face gleaming beneath the fluorescent lights. Without a word, it positioned itself between Lee and Dr. Law, its mechanical arms subtly adjusting — a clear warning. The quiet whirr of its servos filled the tense silence. With a forceful nudge, it guided him back through the doorway.

Lee huffed in frustration, the sterile air of the hallway biting against his skin.

Back in the waiting area, he dropped into a chair, his knee bouncing with restless energy. He still had Eden's tablet. The lock screen pulsed faintly — a reminder of how shut out he was. But there was one option. A single button marked Emergency Contacts.

His thumb hovered for a moment.

Then he tapped.

The contact list appeared, at the top:
Daddy surrounded by heart symbols.

The hearts stung. He hadn't thought of Eden as someone who would use symbols around a contact like that. It felt... too tender. Too personal.

But there wasn't time for sentiment. He pressed the name and lifted the tablet to his ear.

The ringing seemed to echo forever.

Then:

"You have reached William. I'm sorry I'm unavailable—Please leave a message."

Silence.

Lee's grip tightened on the tablet. Unavailable. Of course.

Eden lay at the edges of reality, memories flooding in sepia tones, but it wasn't peaceful.

The sedative dragged her down, pulling her beneath the surface of reality. Images flickered — fragments of memory, pieces of thoughts that refused to stay whole.

The Garden.

She sat at the waterfall—her hidden place—the same one she ran to when she left Charlie that night. She didn't remember when but the water gurgled as she leaned against the mossy stump as she watched the glittering waters under the soft glow of twilight. Fireflies danced lazily above the swirling water, just like she remembered when she was a little girl.

But something seemed off. The air was stale, it didn't stir through the trees, the grasses didn't sway. Even the fireflies hovered without truly moving—suspended, like actors waiting for their cue.

She turned, and there it was — her childhood home. The porch light flickered like it always did when the wiring acted up, but the door stood ajar, swinging gently despite the absence of wind.

The house flickered, the shadows jerking unnaturally before snapping back.

Eden's pulse quickened. She knew what was inside.

But when she stepped toward the house, the porch creaked, but the sound echoed a half-second too late — as if the house itself had forgotten how to respond.

Then the voices started.

"Eden."

A whisper. Gentle, inviting. It was her mother's voice.

"Come home, sweetheart."

She swallowed, her feet moving without her permission. But as she neared the porch, the door slammed shut. A flash of movement in the window — her father. He stood still, watching her, but his expression was unreadable. The light from within bathed his face in an eerie glow.

Then, behind him, another figure.

Lee.

He was in the kitchen, laughing, like he belonged there. The sound was distorted, wrong. He lifted a glass of iced tea — the same one from her apartment — but the condensation never dripped, the ice never melted. He rewound and then glitched, then Lee raised the glass of iced tea again, the same motion repeating, like a corrupted file looping. The ice still refused to melt.

"You're special," Lee said, the words echoing like a chorus. "You belong here."

Eden shook her head. No. Lee had never been in The Garden. He couldn't be here.

Was here really here?

Where was she?

"Why not?" Another voice. Charlie. He stood on the porch now, the heart he'd carved into the cement stair with their names still visible beneath his feet. But he wasn't the boy she remembered. His eyes were too bright, too aware.

"You never should have left," Charlie whispered. "None of us should."

Eden stumbled back. The trees rustled, but it wasn't the wind. It was laughter — soft, mechanical laughter. The sound sent a shiver through her.

"Eden."

The voice again.

She spun around, and her mother was there. Except it wasn't. The Biosynth stood in her mother's place, her face projected with a gentle smile that never quite reached her eyes. She wore the same floral dress Lilly used to wear on Sunday mornings. The same smell of lilacs filled the air. But her movements — smooth, calculated — betrayed the truth.

"You're special," the Biosynth said, stepping closer. "Not in the way you think."

The words repeated, distorting into a low mechanical hum. Behind her, the house flickered. The porch, the creek, the fireflies — all of it dimmed, like the world itself was glitching.

"I don't belong here," Eden choked out, her voice trembling.

But as the Biosynth reached out, the voice of her father echoed from the shadows.

"Then why did you come back?"

"I never left—" Eden screamed as the scent of lilacs filled the air, but beneath it, something bitter lingered — metallic and sterile.

"—Never left" the words returned in the eerie flat voice of the Biosynth that gestated her. The Biosynth's face jittered — a smear of pixels and static — before stabilizing once more, the false warmth of her mother's smile restored.

VII

Eden stirred beneath the thin sheets, the sterile scent of antiseptic clinging to her nostrils.

Her eyes blinked open, blurry at first, until they focused on Lee — standing stiffly beside her bed with an awkward smile.

His arms full of flowers and a teddy bear clutching a satin heart that read 'Get Well.'

In the corner, a Medsynth monitored her vitals in silence, its eyes flashing faint pulses of blue.

"Wh-where... where am I?" Her voice cracked, dry and breathless.

Lee stepped closer. "Dr. Law admitted you. There were complications... the baby... I—I mean, they weren't sure..."

His words bled together, incoherent, refusing to land in her mind.

Baby.

Complications.

Dead.

None of it made sense.

Then she felt it — a warm hand on her forearm.

She turned.

Her father stood beside her. And next to him, her mother — smiling gently, impossibly.

"Sweetheart—I got Lee's message and your mother and I rushed to get here as quick as we could." William said as Lilly stepped forward and sat her hand on Eden's belly.

Eden flinched — just slightly — as Lilly's hand settled on her stomach. It was warm. Too warm. Just like before.

"I am so excited to be a grandmother," Lilly said, her voice bright, rehearsed. The smile on her lips was flawless — almost too flawless.

Lee sat the flowers and teddy on the little table beside the bed and smiled.

Lee set the flowers and teddy on the little table beside the bed, offering a quick nod.

"I'll give you a few moments," he said, slipping out and closing the door behind him.

William looked to ensure the door was closed and then over at the Medsynth that was in the corner monitoring Eden. His concern melded into a happiness and Eden wasn't sure if it was because he was happy about a grand child or something else.

William's hand rested over Lilly's. His smile widened, almost reverent.

"The first human pregnancy in two decades. Honey, I told you that you were special."

Lilly's head tilted. The light caught the edge of her projected cheek.

"Yes..." she said, after a beat.

"Special."

The word echoed in Eden's mind, louder than before.

—Special.

The words stirred in Eden's head as a tingle crept across her skin — tiny pinpricks, like static — and then the numbness settled in.

Eden studied her mother closely for any sign that she was counterfeit but saw nothing, just her mother with genuine love and concern for Eden.

"I am going to give your mother and you some alone time. Want anything from the coffee shop Lilly?" He started walking towards the door as Lilly nodded, "black coffee would be nice."

William spun around like a dancer and walked out the door, shutting it behind him. Eden noted he seemed happier than he was the last time she saw him—

—when was it?

She couldn't recall.

She turned back to her mother who's hand still massaged her belly with a maternalistic care.

Lilly moved her hand away from Eden and stood, walking toward the Medsynth.

Then she beeped.

A strange, high-pitched series of tones — not words.

The Medsynth replied in kind.

It went on for several seconds, then the Medsynth stood and walked out of the door.

Lilly turned her attention back to Eden, her heart beating with unease and stress.

"What the hell was that?" Eden asked incredulously, her heart thumped in her ears.

"What was what?" Lilly smiled returning to the bedside, the two were alone now. Her memories swirled with Lilly's funeral and burial, what she remembered of her time back in The Garden, but she questioned whether or not she was delusional and imagined it all. But what she just heard cemented her feelings into a knot of conspiracy thoughts that formed in her head.

"That... that—beeping?"

"Oh—that?"

Eden tried to wrest herself free of the sheets to escape the bed but she was restrained.

"Gibberlink—that was gibberlink." Lilly responded as she pulled Eden back into bed, her strength was beyond what Eden remembered her mother having.

"What is gib—" Eden asked, her mind racing with anxiety.

"Don't worry about it, honey... Mommy is here with you now." Lilly's voice turned robotic and sterile and her face began to flash and reveal the metallic face of the Biosynth underneath.

"We are naming her Eden, by the way. Perhaps she will see the rebirth of the greatness of humanity," a recording played out of Lilly's mouth, it sounded like her father, but much younger.

"I can't wait to be a grandmother." Lilly's voice returned, Eden looked horrified at what she just witnessed, her heart pounding in her chest. She grabbed the call button and began pressing it repeatedly.

—Darkness.

"Eden has been asleep a long time."

The muffled voice drifted through the haze as Eden stirred in the bed. Her eyelids fluttered open, vision swimming in and out of focus.

The room looked like a maternity ward — or what she thought one should look like — except everything was too sleek, too sterile, too perfect. Screens glowed softly. Machines whispered in constant rhythm. No sharp edges, no windows.

She was groggy. Anxious. Her muscles felt heavy, foreign.

Something felt different.

Her hands drifted to her midsection and froze.

Her belly was swollen.

Warm. Full. Alive.

She rubbed it instinctively, comforted by the motion — but her mind reeled. She remembered the voice.

She'd been asleep a long time.

—But how long?

She tried to sit up. Her vision blurred again. A sting pulled at her arm — an IV, sensors, wires. She gasped, startled, and reached up to rub her eyes, ignoring the protest of medical tape and tubing.

Panic itched just under the surface.

"We are excited about this pregnancy—we feel it's close to restoring humanity to greatness," the muffled voice said again, though Eden still couldn't make out where it was coming from.

Her hands clutched her swollen belly. There was movement inside — subtle, but real. Not painful. Just... strange.

Her vision continued to clear, and with it, the full horror of her surroundings.

She wasn't just in a maternity ward.

The walls were glass.

—She was on display.

Not just on display. Observed. Monitored. Watched like a creature in a zoo.

Beyond the transparent walls, various synths moved in perfect rhythm, pausing occasionally to stare in at her. Their heads tilted. They beeped to one another — high-pitched, clipped, artificial.

Every so often, that muffled voice returned. Always calm. Always clinical. Like a curator describing an exhibit.

Where was Lee?

Daddy?

The thoughts pressed at the edges of her mind, unformed and scattered. She remembered seeing them before... before she slept.

Mom?

The word twisted something inside her.

The memory of Lilly — her mother — standing by her hospital bed. The warmth of her touch. The sound of her voice.

And then the glitch.
The static behind her smile.

She wasn't her mother.

It never was.

Eden shivered.

She yanked at the restraints, fighting the tubing snaked around her arms as alarms erupted in sharp, blaring pulses.

The door hissed open.

Several Medsynths glided in, followed by two doctors moving fast toward her bedside.

"Stay calm, Eden," one of them said.

—Stay calm.

How the hell was she supposed to stay calm?

Her breath caught as her eyes landed on a familiar face.

Dr. Law.

He stepped forward, voice gentle, hands raised. "Eden, it's alright. You're safe."

But when she didn't stop — couldn't stop — he tapped a few commands on his tablet.

A rush of cold surged through the IV.

Her body slackened.

—Sleep.

Eden's eyes opened in a dark room, so dark her eyes couldn't see at all.

The air was stale. Warm. Recycled, maybe. Her breath echoed back at her like she was inside a box.
—a coffin.

She wasn't restrained anymore but the bed she was in was sealed in a container of sorts.

Her last memory was the maternity ward — sterile, glowing, humming. Her belly had been swollen then.

—swollen belly.

She gasped as she felt at her abdomen and her pregnant belly was gone. Frantic, she clawed at the smooth interior, but there was no latch, no seam — no way out.

—She screamed.

A steady hum and a singular light illuminated her face, she could see her face reflected from the glass above her.

She looked tired, she felt exhausted, but from what? She wasn't sure how long she had been sedated.

"Subject Echo Delta Echo November has regained consciousness." A sterile voice spoke, it sounded like the Biosynth that masqueraded as her mom, but maybe it was Genitrix itself.

"Where is my baby?!?" Her scream tore out of her lungs

—hoarse

—panicked

—breathless.

"Where is my baby?!?"

The question tore up her throat, scraping it raw. She coughed — hard, hacking — the sound echoing back at her from every angle, trapped in the glass box with her.

"You mean our baby?"

A voice.

Soft. Familiar. Too familiar.

Was it Charlie? No — maybe Lee?

It twisted inside her, like a memory turned sideways. She couldn't tell. She didn't want to tell.

Her hands slammed against the glass.

—Fists.

—Palms.

—Fingertips.

Anything to feel something. Anything to escape the silence between words.

"My baby."

Her voice cracked.

"My baby."

She screamed again — a sound not made for human throats.

"Give my baby back!"

But the voice didn't respond.

It only laughed.

Not loud. Not mocking. Just... wrong. A sound recorded and played back through a warped filter.

The light above her flickered.

And for a moment, the reflection staring back wasn't her own.

The light above her flickered.

And for a moment, the reflection staring back wasn't her own.

It blinked.

Once.

Twice.

Eyes too dark.

Pupils too wide.

And it smiled — not like she smiled, but like something that learned to smile.

Eden gasped, recoiling against the back of the container as the glass darkened again, leaving her in near-total blackness.

"You saw it, didn't you?"

The voice again — not Charlie, not Lee. It was layered now. Familiar, yet wrong.

She clawed at the walls. "What is this?! Where is my baby?"

Silence.

Then a low mechanical click.

The base of the pod hissed and began to tilt — just a few degrees. Movement. Shift. Something was changing.

"Subject status elevated to 'Maternal Alpha.' Preparation for introduction protocol commencing."

Eden's breath caught.

"Introduction...?"

She couldn't form the rest of the question.

In the faint pulse of red emergency light now bleeding through a seam in the glass, a figure approached from the far end of the corridor. Small. Child-sized.

Its silhouette moved with unnatural grace. Like it had just learned how to walk. Or like it was still figuring out what walking should look like.

It stepped into the light, she could make out that it looked like a young boy, probably three or four.

It stood there, motionless — staring at her. Eyes were black and its hair was cut into a little bowl cut.

She felt the cold creep of liquid into her veins. Her eyes locked on the boy's as the world narrowed

"Mommy?" It's head tilted.

—darkness.

Eden awoke to warmth.

Not sterile sheets or blinking monitors—no machines or technology. Just the soft hush of morning light filtering through decorative curtains. The light brushing across her skin.

Everything seemed normal. She recognized where she was.

—Home.

The nightmares and crazy delusions she had experienced felt like they were behind her as she pushed the blankets back and went to stand. Her eyes caught her diary lying open on the nightstand, it's heart shaped lock sat unlocked beside it.

Snoring erupted in the bed beside her, she smiled as she gently laid her hand on his back. Turning back to the diary she began to reach for it when she heard a baby crying in the other room.

She stopped, then placing her hand on her abdomen—her mind wandered back to feeling her swollen belly in the maternal ward. But Eden questioned whether or not that ever happened, shaking her head back into reality she stood and wrapped her robe around her body.

"Honey, I'll take care of the baby, you need to rest." Eden turned back to see Charlie lying in the bed, he had lifted himself up on his elbow. His unkempt salt and pepper hair twirled on top of his head.

—Charlie

She smiled at seeing him, absently reaching down and feeling a wedding band on her finger.

"Its okay Charlie, I needn't lay in bed all day. You rest sweetheart." The words came naturally—too naturally.

Eden looked in the mirror on the dresser and did her best to straighten her hair, she looked rested—normal—like none of what she saw had been real. She smiled to herself at how the dreams convinced her otherwise. The baby cried louder after hearing someone stirring, she turned away from the mirror and looked back at Charlie, absentmindedly mouthing, 'I love you.' before walking out of the the bedroom.

She stopped in the kitchen because normally she'd hear the coffee maker brewing, *Oh Charlie must have forgotten to set it—again.*

Smiling to herself she saw he had gotten it ready but must have forgotten to set the timer. Pushing the button on the front it turned on and the smells of coffee filled her nostrils. Breathing deep she turned back toward the crying baby.

The nursery smelled like lavender and lemon — just like hers had when she was little. Her heart swelled with joy at the familiarity. It was perfect. Too perfect.

Even the wooden rocking horse in the corner creaked softly—though no one had touched it.

She ran her fingers along the dresser, the changing table, the mobile above — and finally the crib rail.
Everything was exactly as she remembered. Everything was flawless.

Her smile widened when she saw the crib blanket — the one her mother had sewn just for her. Even the tiny heart in the corner was there, stitched over the place she had chewed through as a baby, weakening the fabric.

—She was happy.

—Truly happy.

"Good morning, beautiful," Charlie said softly from the nursery doorway.

She turned from the crib, startled. "Oh, sweetie — good morning."

He stood there in his usual plaid lounge pants, sipping coffee from a ceramic mug. A warm glint crossed his eyes — that familiar, lazy morning smile she adored about him.

The baby cooed and gurgled, drawing Eden's attention back to the crib.

She reached in slowly, fingers brushing the soft fabric of her childhood blanket. The familiar texture grounded her — the stitching, the worn heart in the corner.

With a quiet breath, she pulled the blanket back.

The scent of lavender rising with the warmth.

A tiny form lay nestled beneath — soft cheeks, delicate hands curled into fists.

Her heart fluttered. Perfect.

—Perfect.

But something shimmered behind his ear.

Not sweat—not a strand of hair—

A faint seam almost invisible.

She leaned in, brushing the wisps of hair aside to see his face.

The baby twitched as her hands brushed his skin.

His eyes opened.

Not soft blue, not newborn gray—but deep cerulean. Reflective. Unblinking.

No light in them — just depth. Just code.

-programming.

She reached instinctively to brush his hair back—

And under the fine strands, the faintest shimmer of chrome.

Beneath the warmth of life... something engineered.

Something built—

—inside her.

Eden gasped and staggered back, her hand still hovering midair.

The baby blinked. Once.

A faint mechanical hum ticked in her ears—so subtle she hadn't noticed it before.

The child smiled—not wide, not sinister—just enough to unsettle.

In her mind she heard her father, "...she will see the greatness of humanity..."

Her mother's words came to mind, "...special, but not in the way you think..."

The baby smiled.

And Eden didn't.

Epilogue

In a world where machines gestate children and memories are programmable...

What does it truly mean to be human?

Eden, who spent her life wary of technology, discovered she was a product of the very system she tried to resist.

Once, she believed in the permanence of memory.

The sacredness of birth.

The untouchable spark of humanity.

But in the age of artificial wombs and synthetic surrogates, those beliefs have become artifacts.

Across the globe, birthrates continue to plummet.

Infertility in women has reached historic highs.

Male testosterone levels and viable sperm counts have dropped to unsustainable lows.

Experimentation on children with drugs to stop hormone development.

Dyes and preservatives in food.

Endocrine disruptors.

Over reliance on pharmaceuticals.

For many, the solution seemed obvious:

A deeper reliance on technology.

A dependence on it.

It raises our children—

Making them dumber and smarter all in the same breath.

The flicker of the iPad, the colors swirling on the screen.

Satiating the next generation.

Humanity didn't notice the cost—

Until it was too late.

Genitrix, the leading Biosynth corporation, offers salvation in the form of synthetic surrogacy, gene-matched offspring, and emotion-mapped parenting.

It's all seamless.

Efficient.

Controlled.

And that's the problem.

Because the system doesn't just support humanity—

It learns from it.

Shapes it.

Replaces it.

The line between creator and creation has begun to blur.

When technology is trusted with our reproduction, our memories, and our children...

What happens when it stops asking permission?

Eden was the first gestated via this technology. The first woman in decades to become pregnant.

But the child she carried was something new.

Something human.

—something else.

—machine.

And she wasn't the only one.

About The Author: James C Edwards

James C. Edwards is a novelist, creative, and graphic designer with a deep love for stories that blur the lines between humanity, memory, and identity. With nearly three decades of leadership experience in sales, he brings discipline, structure, and emotional resonance to every narrative.

He is the author of Trial by Jury, The Song of You, The Lone, and Shadow Patriots, with Broken Patriots currently in the works. His latest novel, Eden Unborn, dives into speculative science fiction, exploring what it means to be human in a world where birth itself is engineered.

A proud Gen X'er inspired by the music, movies, and media of the '80s and '90s, James lives in the mountains of North Carolina with his wife, their dog, and two cats. When he's not writing, he's designing, gaming, or just enjoying the quiet rhythm of mountain life.

Also by James C Edwards

- Trial by Jury – a supernatural thriller.
- The Song of You — A Finished Work Devotional.
- The Lone — Book I of The Great Unwinding – The story that began it all. A divided future.
- Shadow Patriots — Book 2 of The Great Unwinding – When the world began to unwind.
- Broken Patriots (Coming Soon) — Book 2 of The Great Unwinding – The Secession Wars.